World of R...

A 3-in-1 Listen-Along Re...

Disney
MICKEY
& FRIENDS

3 Tales of Fun

Printed in the United States of America
Mickey's Birthday First Edition, March 2013
Huey, Dewey, and Louie's Rainy Day First Edition, March 2014
A Perfect Picnic First Edition, April 2013
First Bind-up Edition, September 2016
1 3 5 7 9 10 8 6 4 2
Library of Congress Control Number: 2016936338
FAC-029261-16204
ISBN 978-1-4847-9034-2
For more Disney Press fun, visit www.disneybooks.com

SUSTAINABLE
FORESTRY
INITIATIVE

Certified Sourcing

www.sfiprogram.org
SFI-01415

Mickey's Birthday

By Elle D. Risco
Illustrated by the Disney Storybook Artists
and Loter, Inc.

DISNEP PRESS
Los Angeles • New York

Mickey woke up
and jumped out of bed.
"Good morning, Pluto," he said,
like he did every day.

Mickey ate breakfast,
like he did every day.

He did his stretches,
like he did every day.

But today was not like
every other day.
Today was Mickey's birthday!
"What should we do today?"
Mickey asked Pluto.

Mickey looked out the window
and saw his friends.
They were walking along the path
behind his house.
I wonder what they are doing,
thought Mickey.

Mickey looked closer.

Donald was carrying cups and plates.

Daisy was carrying lemonade.

Goofy was carrying
a bunch of balloons.

Minnie was carrying a big cake.

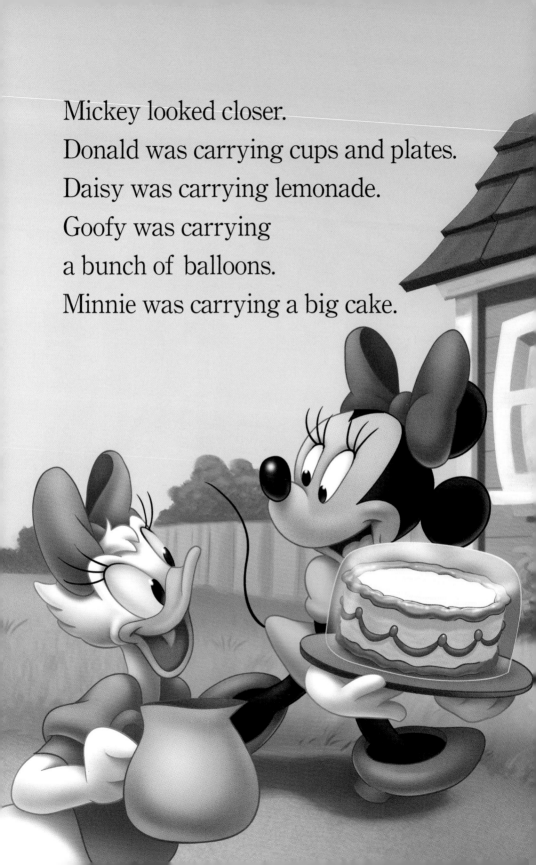

"Pluto!" Mickey said.
"It looks like they are having a party!
Do you think it could be a birthday
party . . . for me?"

"We'd better get dressed!" he said,
"just in case!"
So Mickey dusted off his gloves
and polished his buttons.

He even brushed Pluto.
Finally, they were ready.

A little later, the doorbell rang.

Ding, dong!

Mickey opened the door.

It was Donald, and he looked upset.

"What's wrong, Donald?"

Mickey asked.

"My favorite hammock is broken,"
Donald said.
"I cannot nap without it.
Can you help me fix it?"
"Sure, Donald!" said Mickey.

So Mickey went with Donald.
As they walked, an idea
popped into Mickey's head.
Maybe Donald is <u>really</u> taking me
to my party! he thought.

Mickey was so excited that
he started to skip.

Donald stopped
near two large trees.
He looked down at the ground.
There was the broken hammock.

Mickey looked around.
There were no balloons and no cake.
There was just one friend
who needed his help.
So Mickey helped Donald
fix his hammock.

"Thanks, Mickey!" Donald said
when it was fixed.
Then Donald climbed
into the hammock and fell asleep.
"You're welcome," Mickey said,
and he started to head home.

On the way, he met Minnie and Daisy.

"Mickey!" Minnie said.

"We have something to show you!"

So Mickey went with them.

Oh boy, thought Mickey.

Are <u>they</u> taking me to my party?

Minnie and Daisy led Mickey
to their flower garden.
"Ta-da!" said Daisy.
"Everything is blooming!"
said Minnie.

Mickey looked around.
The flowers are pretty, but
where is my party? Mickey wondered.
"Do you want to help us garden?"
Daisy asked him.
So Mickey helped water the flowers.

A few minutes later, Goofy ran up
and pulled Mickey away.
"Mickey! Mickey!" Goofy shouted,
tugging on his friend's arm.
"You have to see this!"

So Mickey went with Goofy.
Goofy seems very excited,
Mickey thought.
He <u>must</u> be taking me to my party.

"Look, Mickey!" Goofy said,
stopping by a large rock.
Mickey looked all around,
but there was no sign of a party.
Why was Goofy so excited?

Then Mickey looked down.

Two snails were racing on the rock.

"Gosh! Watch 'em go!" Goofy said.

Mickey had never seen a snail race.

It was exciting,

but not as exciting as a party.

Mickey watched for a while.
Then he and Pluto headed home.
"Oh well, Pluto," Mickey said.
"I guess I was wrong.
I guess there is no
birthday party after all."

Mickey walked up the
path to his house.
He opened his front door
and stepped inside.
As he felt for the light switch . . .

"SURPRISE!"

His friends jumped out at him.

It was a surprise party for Mickey!

For the first time all day,

Mickey had not expected it!

He was so surprised!
"I do not understand," said Mickey.
"How did you make a party
at my house?
And in secret?"

"Hyuck," Goofy laughed.
"We are pretty sneaky!"
Minnie giggled.
"We took turns
keeping you busy," she said.

Mickey thought about his day.
Donald's broken hammock.
Daisy and Minnie's flowers.
Goofy's snail race.
Now Mickey understood.

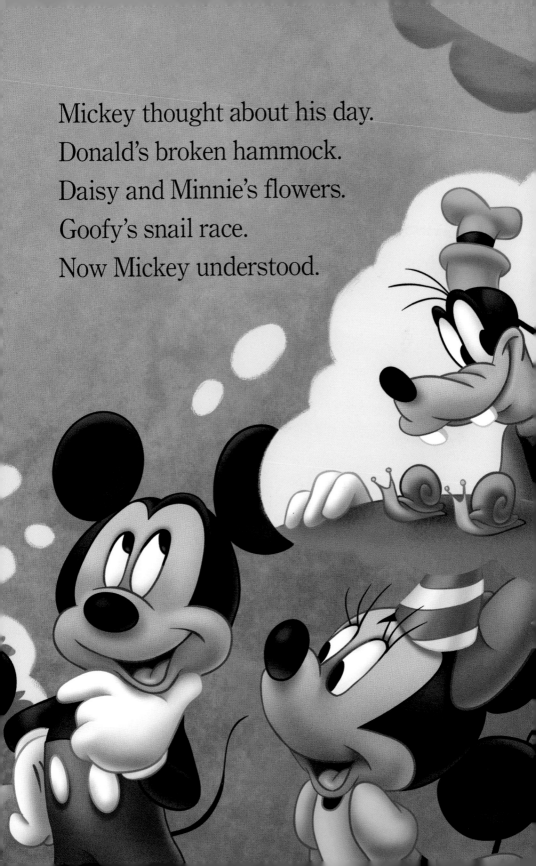

Mickey smiled a huge smile.
"Thanks, everyone," he said,
"for the best party ever!"
His friends clapped and cheered,
"Happy birthday, Mickey!"

Huey, Dewey, and Louie's Rainy Day

By Kate Ritchey
Illustrated by the Disney Storybook Art Team
and Loter, Inc.

DISNEP PRESS
Los Angeles • New York

Huey, Dewey, and Louie were excited.
They were planning to
surprise Uncle Donald!

The boys loved to
visit their uncle.
He had a big backyard and
lots of toys to play with.
But their favorite part of visiting
was playing with Donald.

Huey rang the doorbell.
"Hiya, Uncle Donald!" they shouted
when he opened the door.
"Oh, hello, boys," said Donald.
"I was just getting ready
to read the newspaper."

Huey and Dewey
pushed past Donald.
"Did you get any new toys?"
asked Huey.
"What kind of snacks do you have?"
asked Dewey.

Louie grabbed his uncle's arm.
"Come play with us, Uncle Donald,"
he said.
But Donald just wanted
to read his paper.

"Let's go play in the backyard!"
Huey said.
He swung open the back door.
Suddenly . . .

CRASH! BOOM!

Lightning flashed in the windows.
Thunder rumbled through the house.

"Oh, no!" the boys cried.
"We cannot go outside now!
What are we going to do?"

"We could play a game," Dewey said.
"I will be blue!"
"I am red!" said Huey.
"I will be green!" said Louie.
"You can be yellow, Uncle Donald."

The boys played three games.

Dewey won every time.

Donald was <u>not</u> having fun!

"Maybe we should do something else,"
said Huey.

"How about painting?" said Louie.
He found paint and paintbrushes
in the closet.
"You can hang our pictures
on the wall,"
Huey told Donald.

Donald thought painting
was too messy.
"Why don't you boys have
some hot chocolate?" he said.
"I am going to
read the newspaper."

The boys watched the rain
and listened to the thunder.
"There must be something fun
we can do," said Huey.

The boys looked at Donald.

He had fallen asleep in his chair.

"I have a great idea!" Dewey said.

"Let's build a fort."

The brothers gathered sheets,
towels, blankets, and pillows.
They took cushions from the couch
and chairs from the kitchen.

Soon construction began
on the fort!

Huey built a lookout tower
to spy on anyone
outside the fort.

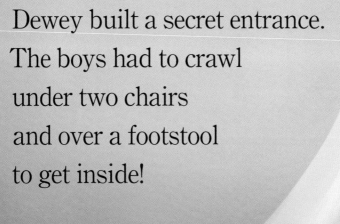

Dewey built a secret entrance.
The boys had to crawl
under two chairs
and over a footstool
to get inside!

Louie was in charge of supplies.
He piled up everything
the boys would need.

Donald was still sleeping.
He did not know that
the boys were building around him.

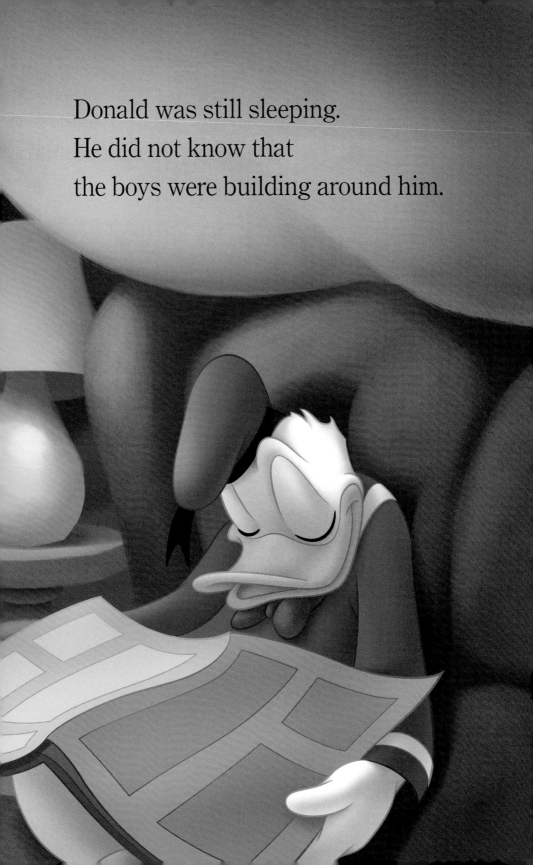

At last, Fort McDuck was complete!
The main room was big
with lots of space to camp out.
The lookout let the boys
watch for invaders.

The fort's kitchen had
all kinds of snacks.
And the secret entrance was
so well hidden
no one would ever find it!

Suddenly, thunder boomed
through the fort's walls.
"We are being attacked!"
yelled Huey.

Huey, Dewey, and Louie
bravely defended Fort McDuck.
"Hooray!" they yelled.
"The fort is safe!"

All the cheering woke up Donald.
He opened his eyes to find that he
was surrounded by pillows and sheets.
"What is going on?" he asked.

"Do not worry, Uncle Donald,"
said Louie.
"We saved you from the invaders
attacking Fort McDuck!" Dewey added.

"Hey!" said Huey from the lookout.

"The rain has stopped."

"Now can we go play outside?"
Dewey asked Donald.

"I think that is a great idea!"
said Donald.

The boys crawled out of the fort.
They put on their
rain boots and coats.
Donald stayed inside the fort,
where it was quiet.
Now he could read his newspaper.

"Hooray!" shouted Huey, Dewey, and Louie as they jumped into the rain puddles. It was the perfect ending to their day at Uncle Donald's house!

A Perfect
Picnic

By Kate Ritchey
Illustrated by Loter, Inc. and
the Disney Storybook Artists

Los Angeles • New York

It was a beautiful spring day.
The sun was shining and
the birds were singing.
Mickey and Pluto were planning
a picnic in the park.

"I have an idea," Mickey said.
"We should invite our friends
to the picnic!
We can all enjoy the sunshine
and share our favorite foods!"

Mickey called Goofy.
"Pluto and I are having a picnic,"
he told his friend.
"Would you like to come?"
Goofy agreed. A picnic was a
great way to spend the day!

"Bring your favorite fruit,
your favorite sandwich,
and your favorite drink,"
Mickey said.
"Then everyone can trade baskets."

Next, Mickey visited Minnie.
"We are having a picnic,"
he told her.
Minnie was excited.
She could not wait
to share her favorite foods!

Soon, Mickey found Donald and Daisy.
"A picnic sounds like a great idea,"
Daisy said.
"I know just what to make!"
Donald added.

At home, Donald started his lunch.
He took out two pieces of bread
to make a sandwich.
He got out his favorite drink.
Then he chose a piece of fruit.

But as he looked at the food,
Donald began to get hungry.
I do not <u>want</u> to share my lunch,
he thought.
I want to eat it myself!

Minnie was making lunch, too.
She put her drink into a jug.
She packed a piece of fruit.
Then she made her
favorite sandwich,
peanut butter!

As she got ready,
Minnie started to wonder
if she would like the other lunches.
I do not <u>want</u> to share my lunch,
she thought.
I want to eat it myself!

Daisy was excited about sharing
her lunch with her friends!
She hummed to herself as she
packed her sandwich and drink.
Then she picked up a banana.

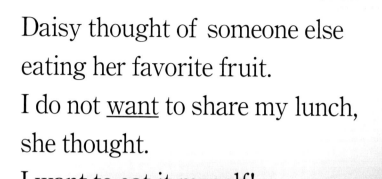

Daisy thought of someone else
eating her favorite fruit.
I do not <u>want</u> to share my lunch,
she thought.
I want to eat it myself!

Over at Goofy's house,
the kitchen was very messy!
Goofy was making lemonade
to take to the picnic.
He was soaking wet and
covered in lemon juice!

Goofy tasted his lemonade.
It was delicious!
This is my best lemonade ever,
he thought.
I do not <u>want</u> to share it.
I want to drink it all by myself!

Mickey did not know that his friends
had changed their minds.
He was busy packing his basket.
"Is that everything, Pluto?"
he asked.

Pluto barked and whined.
"Thanks for reminding me,"
Mickey said.
"I would not want
to forget your lunch!"

Mickey finished filling his basket
and went to the park.
As he walked,
he sang to himself.

Mickey's friends were
waiting for him.
They all had baskets of food.
But they did not look happy.

"What is wrong?" Mickey asked.
"I do not want to share my lunch,"
Donald said.
"What if I do not like
the lunch I get?" Minnie asked.

Daisy and Goofy agreed.
Everyone wanted to eat
their own favorite foods.
"I guess we do not <u>have</u> to trade,"
Mickey said.

Minnie looked at Mickey.
He looked very sad.
She handed him her basket.
"I will trade with you, Mickey,"
she said.

Mickey's friends saw that
Minnie had made Mickey happy.
They wanted to make Mickey happy, too.
"Will someone trade with me?"
Donald asked, holding out his lunch.
Soon, they had all swapped baskets.

Mickey laid out a blanket.

Minnie passed out plates.

Goofy handed out napkins.

Daisy gave everyone a cup.

Donald set out forks.

Finally, it was time to eat!

Mickey opened his basket first.
He started to laugh.
Donald looked in his basket
and laughed, too.
Everyone had packed lemonade
and peanut butter sandwiches!

But each basket had a different fruit.
Donald had a pineapple.
Daisy had grapes.
Minnie had an orange.
Goofy had a banana.
Mickey had an apple.

"How can we share our fruit?"
Minnie asked.
"I have an idea," Mickey said.
"Leave it to me!"

While everyone ate their sandwiches
and drank their lemonade,
Mickey cut up the fruit.
He put it all in a bowl
and mixed it together.

It was a big fruit salad!
Now everyone could try
their friends' favorite fruits.
"What a great way to share
what we like best," Daisy said.

Mickey's friends agreed
as they ate their dessert.
It was the perfect end
to a perfect picnic!